One Step At A Time

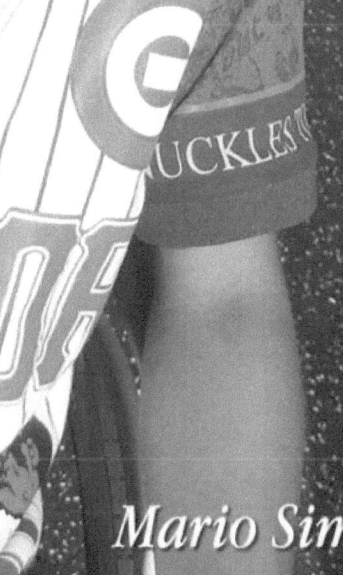

Mario Simmons

One Step At A Time

Mario Simmons

Dedication

To my parents, and the friends and family who supported me when I was down. This is for you.

Acknowledgment

There are so many people I need to thank. People who supported me when I was at my lowest, and who encouraged me to write out my experiences in the form of this memoir. I have to acknowledge, first and foremost, my family: my mother and father, my two brothers, my grandparents and cousins, and all the uncles and aunts who did everything they could to decrease my discomfort. I love you all.

Thank you also, to the friends who stood by me when others fled. I will always remember what you did for me. I'm grateful to my editors and publishers for helping me produce this book, as well as to all the friends and family who read through the manuscript and helped me better it. Finally, I thank you, the reader, for your time reading my book. In times of difficulty, I pray you find some help within it.

About the Author

Mario Simmons is a family man through and through, with a passion for sports that runs deep in his veins. When he's not cheering on his favorite team, he's writing about his own experiences with pain and depression, in the hopes that it will inspire and motivate other young people.

Preface

This book is a labor of both pain and love. I have delved deep into the most heart-breaking of my experiences in an attempt to produce a work that inspires anyone in the same shoes.

Contents

Page Blank Left Intentionally

Chapter 1- The Beginning

The amount of happiness that parents feel at the birth of a child is incomparable. There are also many other emotions that are felt – joy, elation, pride, determination, and much more. These emotions regarding the momentous event, directed toward the child and the parents, changes their lives forever. Every parent wants the best for their children and fights hard in life for this. Of course, no mommy or daddy can say what the fate of their beloved child will turn out to be. They can never know whether the child would lead a happy, successful life or end up with problems they are unable to maneuver.

The same can be said about my parents. They had no idea of what I would have to go through as I grew up. They were two of the happiest people on the face of the earth on June 21, 1997, when I came into the world - their third, beloved son named Mario Simmons. These wonderful human beings welcomed me just like they had embraced my two elder brothers before me, Marcus and Melvin Jr. My parents lived in breezy West Palm Beach, Florida, with the three of us and their extended family scattered all around the town. Those were happier times when things were simpler and everyone seemed to know everyone else. We were a close-knit community, where everyone's kids were treated like one's own, whether it was about dinner or a whip on the butt. I had one of those childhoods where children are lavished with love and consideration. Our parents doted on us three brothers. If it were up to my dad, he would give us everything in the world. All we had to do was get the words out of our mouth. My mother, likewise, could not have been more devoted to her sons and husband. It was one happy family, without any negativity or strife. It was like we had been blessed with our personal heaven on earth. During those days, it seemed like nothing could shatter this bubble we lived in. Oh, how wrong we were!

Since I was the youngest, it was not only my parents who gave special preference to me, but my brothers were also the same. They would always look out for me, and unlike other elderly siblings, who tend to shun their younger brothers and sisters aside or ignore them, they would involve me in everything they did. From playing games on the gaming console to joining them in physical activities, I had been a part of their group every time. I realize now what a blessing that was because when I notice families these days, that bond or consideration toward the feelings of others is desperately missing. It is both sad and deplorable, but society, media, and technology have really torn family and cultures apart. In our case, it was not only my immediate family that was so closely tied together, but my extended family was also as much a part of our everyday lives as we siblings or our parents were for each other. We even had neighbors who were almost our family - they were that close. This perhaps is one thing that mystifies me, how people are willing to let go of real relationships for inanimate objects like their phones and other mobile devices.

My brothers and I would spend entire days on our Nintendo 64, playing our favorite game, Mario Kart - the one I share my name with. But this was not the only activity we indulged in. When we weren't holed up in the house playing Mario or Double 007, we would be outside running wild, involving ourselves in games like manhunt, basketball, or even football.

I have to admit that as much as Nintendo was a favorite, nothing was comparable with going outside and playing in the wind under the clear sky. It made me feel truly alive. This perhaps was the reason why our dad would ensure that we visited the Palm Beach Mall at least three times a week after school. On Friday nights, Melvin, my eldest brother, would take Marcus and me to his football games, where we would either watch from the sidelines or sometimes be invited to play with them. This is where I believe I developed my passion for sports. After the football matches, we would always head toward McDonald's for a meal. Of course, since this trip included all of my brothers' friends, I would almost always be the youngest person. My ability to blend in with adults started at this point, and this is why I've never had trouble communicating with anyone, be they younger or older than me. I was too used to this set-up since I was a little kid.

Whenever the weekend began, it would be a reason for the family to visit and spend time with extended family. Both my brothers and I would head off to our aunt's house where we would team up with our cousins to have battles of Nintendo games. Since all of us had our own controllers, it meant that nobody had to wait their turn and everyone could play at the same time. I would generally be teamed with one of my cousins while Marcus would partner with the other cousin. I have to admit that I was extremely competitive, but never a sore loser.

No matter how many times my cousin and I lost, we would never get bitter about it, even though we would fight as hard as we could. Saturday nights meant movie nights for all us cousins. We would hang out at a local cinema, Muvico, in the city to catch the most thrilling movie of the week. The place with its dark gloom was exotic for us. It was never dangerous, of course, but the guy who ran the place was rather eccentric.

Sunday nights, on the other hand, were meant for a huge dinner at home that my aunt and dad would prepare. The cousins and I were sent out in the backyard to play football. It was a tradition that we followed for the longest time. I still reminisce about it. Just the thought of those warm, balmy nights brings a smile to my face. Ahhh, the charm of those golden days!

Whenever the week began, it would be rather a grumpy start. Mondays are bad, especially for kids who don't want to leave the comfort and coziness of home for cold classrooms. Even though I hated going back on Mondays, the school remained one of my most favorite places. I didn't only enjoy the company of my friends, but I also had a good connection with my teachers. What's more, Monday would be slightly better because I would always discuss our Sunday football games with my friends. As I said before, my interest in sports, particularly the Sunday matches made a huge impact on my year as a 4th grader. Upon the encouragement of my family, I decided to start practicing basketball before the start and end of school each day. By the time tryouts started, I had practiced enough to have the courage to apply for the school basketball team. I gave the practice session my all and fortunately secured a position on the team. My parents were so proud the day I got my jersey with number 3 etched on its back.

Being a point guard, I had played well till the last game, by accumulating 12 points, five assists, and two steals. The season ended as well as I had hoped, but I never stopped practicing, because after all, practice makes a man perfect. In the coming year, I was expecting everything to change, as it was going to be middle school and I would be turning into a teenager. The excitement was real!

My parents were very careful with how they raised us. I was given a lot of responsibilities when I became a teenager. From setting my alarm clock for school, to ironing my clothes, to walking to the bus stop all by myself, I was made to feel like a grownup so that I would become more responsible and careful with my own care.

The next year I shifted to Roosevelt Middle from Bear Lakes Middle. This is the place where I came across a very good friend who I had lost when we were in elementary school. Even though we had tried keeping in touch before, it had become impossible after some time and we had ended up losing all contact. But in middle school we reunited again. It wasn't long before we were able to rekindle our old comradeship and it got so strong that we became the best of friends.

Our teachers would claim how one was never seen without the other. Wherever Mario went, Trevor would also appear and vice versa. Good times pass swiftly and the same happened to my time in middle school. It passed in a haze of hanging out with friends, driving around the town on my little bike, eating, and shopping as much as we possibly could. The time was fast approaching when I had to prepare for high school.

My parents had already prepared me for this, telling me how high school was going to be harder and more grueling than anything I had ever seen before. Luckily enough, my worst fears were laid to rest during the first week of high school. I realized it wasn't as difficult as everyone seemed to have made it out to me. Yes, the studies were harder, but if you decided to work hard, things could be managed well. It has to be stated that I was extremely fortunate to come across some really good friends in high school, who became the reason for my contentment. I was fast turning into a player. I won't lie and rather say this was something completely extraordinary because it had been coming on for the longest time. Girls always seemed to flock around me and high school was no different. But that is not where my luck ended, I was also very well-liked by my teachers and juniors. My friends, Trevor, Katlyn, Stacy, and Tiffany would hang out in our cars over the weekend.

Another group of high school friends would join us, doing stunts in our cars, and living life to the absolute fullest. This, I feel, is the reason why I loved the 10th grade so much. This love that I seemed to garner everywhere followed me to my first job at McDonald's. All the people there seemed to love me for who I was. It was like I was living in my fairytale, where everything was perfect without the presence of any villain. Life simply couldn't get better. Of course, it could get worse! It was only a glorious two months later that everything took a 180-degree turn.

What changed the lives of my immediate and extended family forever was the murder of one of my female cousins. It was merely a few short hours before that I had been hanging out with her, talking about her daughter's expected visit. Anyhow, I tried to keep my feelings under control for her daughter, who would need all the emotional support she could have. I wanted to be there for her which is why I made sure that no anger or sorrow escaped my soul into the real world.

I had to be strong for her and comfort her on losing her mother. It was devastation like nothing I had ever seen in my life before. This was the first incident that opened my eyes to the cruelty and harshness of life. From being a naive young boy, I suddenly matured overnight. It was like a bang to the head that makes you accept that life is not all fun and games, it is more vicious than we can ever imagine it to be.

Even though such a long time has passed, even today, after all these years, I can't forget the happy, shining face of my cousin. She had broken up with her husband, and he didn't want anybody else with her but him, so one night he kicked her door down and barged into the house. The demented man brought her downstairs and shot her in back of the head. She was 42 years old. Justice was served when the police arrested him and five years later, he was sentenced to life in jail. I cannot forget how excited she was that day about her daughter visiting, and how she couldn't stop smiling for the pure joy that comes to a parent's face when they watch their child grow up. I remember all the good times that I had spent with her, so many memories built together. I badly wish that I could have just one more day with her and absorb her warmth and love once again. But no one has ever returned from death, and no matter how much I wish it, she will never be back with that beautiful smile of her.

Life always goes on, no matter what kind of tragedy strikes, and so it did. I graduated from high school with good grades and decided to move out of my parents' house. I couldn't burden them with my responsibility forever, so I started looking for my own place and found one in just the right neighborhood, where my grandparents lived.

Every time I had to reach my house, I would need to pass theirs. This meant that I would often see my grandfather sitting in the lawn, watching his favorite show on his portable TV. It always gave me pleasure looking at him, sitting with an air of calm, completely tuned into the program he would be watching. There were many times I would stop by their house to offer to clean up my granddad's garage. I used to do that for a very long time, as it not only allowed me to spend some hours with the beloved old man but also let me discover some real treasures among his precious collections. Now that all of us have grown up, some of the traditional family events have changed. On Friday nights, my family gathers at my grandparents' house to watch Heat games and consume fish and fries. This was mainly because my grandmother was a huge fan of sports, baseball in particular, and loved watching Florida Marlins. They were always her favorite team, and she refused to listen to any criticism about them. She was a proud and independent woman, my grandmother.

I remember that when I first found a job, she was the one who was the proudest. She couldn't stop looking at me with pride, or praising my efforts in front of the rest of the family. It was she who instilled the importance of earning your own money within me. According to her, there was simply nothing more important than taking care of your family, be it emotionally or financially. Even though I used to laugh at that time, I understood exactly what she meant as I grew up. I realized that it is money that helps the world go round and without it, we are all helpless and powerless.

I had planned to save as much money as possible for me and then open up my own store that would sell shoes and clothes. My grandmother, as well as other family members, supported me wholeheartedly on this decision. But saving money is a concept that is easier said than done. I'm still trying to save enough money.

Once I completed my high school and graduated with good grades, I started my new job at a Lexus dealership. This meant that I had to work at two places for seven days a week. Even though I was absorbed in work and busy all the time, I still made sure that I took out time as often as possible to spend with family and friends. I knew they were the ones who gave me happiness and kept me going. I never wanted to let them go. My life, even though it had seen tragedy closely and personally, had gotten back to the phase where life was good.

I had my loved ones, my job was stable and paid ok - things were settled. I was happy and the people around me were happy too. What I have learned from my time and experience is that life is full of unexpected twists and turns, some worse than others. My life still has a long way to go, with many wrong turns to take, but I am sure that in compensation, there will also be many right ones.

A balance is always maintained, even though we are not able to see it from time to time in our happiness or misery. These are the times when a change comes, and the world as we know it shatters. Things turn a somersault, but what I wish to stress is that they do go back to being settled and content. You only have to give it some time and things do change for the better, even if it seems inconceivable at that moment.

One such thing turned my entire world upside down forever. I never thought it could happen, never thought something like this could happen to me. But it did and it knocked the breath out of me. I stumbled so hard that for some time, it seemed that I would never be able to get back up or piece my life together again. I know I gave up on many things, but I refused to let one incident, albeit a life-changing one, bring me down. It was through sheer determination that I overcame all my troubles.

Chapter 2- The Day Everything Changed

Things happen for a reason, but we don't always see that reason while we're in the situation. Something similar happened to me. As I mentioned earlier, something completely unexpected happened to me that neither I nor anyone else could have ever predicted. Here is how my life took a 180-degree turn. I woke up as the alarm rang and prepared myself to get to work like every other day. I went to work, completed my assigned tasks, and left for home, not knowing what was in store for me.

I decided to head to my girlfriend's house before heading home, just to see her. I spent some quality time with her and kissed her goodnight. When I left, I decided to walk slowly and savor the beautiful night. There was no worry and nothing negative in my mind. Life had been treating me well.

Just as I was on the street where my home was, I heard a loud bang that sounded too terrifyingly like a gunshot. The sound came first and then came the burning pain. I had been shot in the back and couldn't register this had happened. When I turned, I saw to my horror that it was my own first cousin, from my dad's side. He ran away the instant he realized his shot had hit the right target. People started coming out of the door, wondering what was going on. But I was too shocked to even think straight. What had happened? Why had my own cousin shot me? What had I ever done to deserve this? All these thoughts flashed through my head within a few seconds, before I blacked out due to the sheer torture my body was experiencing. Even though a lot of time has passed since the actual incident, I still cannot forget the loud bang. I can distinctly recall the haunting memory of that piercing bullet, and me falling on my side.

I was very lucky that the shot was not fatal, and that it didn't pierce any major organs. But by no means was it a casual injury. It damaged my spine to the point that I sustained L1/L2 spinal cord injury (SCI). But it was only later that I was to know just how much damage the shooting had actually done on my body. In only a few minutes, there was an ambulance standing right next to me and medics had loaded me up and put me on drips. The pain was like fire lapping at me so intensely that I blacked out before too many thoughts could crowd my head.

The next time I opened my eyes, I was in a hospital and my girlfriend was standing beside me with tears in her eyes, looking petrified. I couldn't feel my legs or have any kind of sensation below my waist. When I exclaimed that I couldn't feel anything, tears started rolling down her cheeks. That was the point when my father rushed into the room, calling for the nurse at the same time.

Neither the nurse nor my father answered any of my questions and I spiraled back into darkness, as morphine was injected into the drips attached to my body. This became my reality for some time. The minute I would wake up, a nurse would give me a dose of morphine so that I did not have to experience any pain. Whenever I would wake up, my mom would be around, looking terrified, but assuring me that everything would be ok and that I should not worry about a single thing.

I was too numb to form any proper thoughts except for what had happened. After a while, I was allowed to stay awake for longer than a few seconds. It was then that I asked all my questions. I was gently told by the doctors that because of where I had been shot, my spine had experienced a rupture. Because of this, I was unable to feel anything below the waist. I would be kept in the ICU and then shifted to the room for as long as the doctors thought it was necessary to recover. Luckily, the shot hadn't been fatal, but it had done extensive damage to my body. The police came in to question me about why I thought I had been shot. I told them that I had no idea why my cousin had gotten resentful enough to shoot me. Nobody had any reasonable answer to the question and the police left just as bewildered as they had come.

When I think about it now, I feel it must have been because I had been doing well in life and continuously progressing. Not only had I completed my high school education but was also working two jobs, hoping to join college soon. He must have become so jealous that his anger had resulted in him shooting me. When I was given my phone back, I saw that nobody had forgotten me. There were dozens of messages and calls from friends as well as family.

As soon as I was transferred from the ICU to my room, visits from my loved ones began. This is the one thing that kept me going, and my hope strong. It made me realize just how blessed I was, and that there were so many people who cared enough to visit and call every single day. The worst days of this torture I spent were when I was in the ICU. It wasn't that I wasn't well cared for. It was simply the fact that

I hated being fed through the tube and hearing the machine beeping all the time. The care I was getting at the hospital was actually amazing. Doctors would come in twice a day to check up on me, and the nurses were there around the clock. They would arrive instantly when I pushed the help button. I was given pain medication the second I asked for it because the doctors understood my pain was really bad.

Since I was being fed through the tube, I was given my diet in portions. This was one of the worst things that I experienced at the hospital - I missed eating regular food. I would pray to God all the time that the tube would come out so that I was able to enjoy normal food again like before. It wasn't long before my prayers were answered, and the doctors told me that I had been making excellent progress and was being removed from the ICU.

I was extremely proud of myself because I hadn't given in to the depression of what was going on. I was handling everything really well considering that my circumstances were so very difficult. The next day, I saw the nurses bring a moveable bed into my room. I was overwhelmed with happiness, as this meant I was being shifted to another room, where there would be no bleeping machines, and I wouldn't need to be fed through a tube. I was finally getting rid of the detested ICU! They shifted me to another room and the doctors informed me that I would be able to have regular food. The first thing I had was a meal from Popeye's. My girlfriend brought it for me on my request. I used to love it but to my surprise, I realized that even eating more than three mouthfuls was difficult. Since I had been on portion control and fed intravenously for so long, I had completely lost my appetite. My girlfriend had to force me to eat, as the food did not taste the same to me anymore.

It got to the point that the doctors had to give me medication in order to make me hungry. Even after that, it took some time to build up proper eating habits again. It's truly ironic as when I was on the tube, I could dream of little else than eating normal food, but the minute I was allowed it, all hunger vanished and I could barely nibble on what was given to me.

But thankfully, the medication worked and I regained my appetite. I have to mention again how amazing the nursing staff of the hospital was. They literally were the ones who brought me back from the dead. Had it not been their consideration, motivation, and dedicated help, I would never have been able to make it through. They made me comfortable in all the ways possible and would be there whenever I needed their aid or assistance. The minute I pushed the button, someone would come to check on me, making sure I was given whatever I required, from medicine to physical assistance in turning and whatnot. They never failed to respond in time, no matter what time of the day or night it was. It is something I will forever be grateful for. It was also the nurses who first took me out in the open when I had recovered well enough and been shifted to a room. The first breath of fresh air that I took was like being born again.

The exhilaration I experienced was one like nothing I had ever felt before. The sun, the open air and the light breeze all combined together made me heady. I did not want to go back in but I was only meant to stay outside for the briefest of time and was too soon returned to the room. But while I was out, I breathed in deep to retain the smell and the feel of the outside.

Let me tell you what it feels like to be out of the hospital. It's like you are finally free after years of captivity, even if it has only been days. And for a person like me, who likes nothing better than spending his days in the outdoors, this blessing was too real. Once I was shifted to my room and started taking food by mouth, it was time to move on with my recovery session. This meant regular rehabilitation. I don't think I have ever gone through anything more difficult than learning to get back on my feet. When I look back, I think of all the efforts parents put in trying to make their little ones walk. They guide them, show them how it's done, and motivate as well as encourage them with praises on the smallest of progresses. My case was pretty much the same. The only different thing was that I had to teach myself. As my doctors kept reminding me over and over again, nobody other than me could do this and there was no one who could motivate me like myself. The first time I hit the rehabilitation center, I could not even work out on the cardio machine for 45 minutes straight. It was not only difficult, but painful too.

However, I had made up mind to not give in to the terrible blight afflicting me, and to put in my best efforts no matter what. This was the reason that by the second day of rehab, I was able to end my first half with surprising performance and speed. The therapist saw my potential and dedication, and so gave me extra attention. He encouraged me to get on a flatbed and try to turn my side myself, without any aid. This may sound easy, but for someone who cannot feel anything below the waist, it required herculean efforts. However, I kept at it until I was able to master it within a few sessions.

But let me stress, it was by no means easy. It hurt, and just the thought that I was reduced to these simple tasks was demotivating enough to put anyone through extreme depression. Throughout the entire rehab session, however, I made sure that I never missed a day. No matter how bad it hurt or how terrible I felt afterward, I went to every session and tried to accomplish everything the therapist asked of me.

When the pain became too much or I was too exhausted, the therapist would understand that it was one of those days when I needed a less-rigorous workout, and would offer to massage my legs in order to elevate the pain I was experiencing. The massages did not only help lessen the pain, but also strengthened my leg muscles. The nurses who massaged me were excellent at their job, and their hands would work magic on my lower body as they got all the painful knots out.

When I was approaching the end of my rehab sessions, I decided that it would be best for me to directly get into physical therapy. There was no point in delaying it. The doctors thought that since my body was already reacting so well to rehab, it would be able to handle the stress of physical therapy well. I trusted their judgment as they had only given the best possible advice so far, which is why I opted for it immediately. I have to tell you that life wasn't very easy for me in those days. Later, I will talk in more detail about the emotional struggles I went through when dealing with the repercussions of my shooting, but I would like to mention a few things here. It is when you are at your lowest that you learn about your potential as well as the reality of the people in your life. I experienced something similar. I saw many loved ones turn into strangers and quite a few strangers become amazing friends who have been better than family. I discovered that the only person you can ultimately rely on is you. If you don't motivate yourself, no one else is going to take that role and responsibility for you.

What else? You have more strength than you ever knew. I never thought I would be able to come out of such an experience alive and whole, but here I am, telling you my tale myself. If you had seen what the shooting had done to me, you would never have believed this was possible. With the love and support of a few people in my life, I have been able to make a recovery that is miraculous in itself. Things were so dark at one point that all I wanted to do was end everything. But life refuses to snuff out that easily and hence, I am still alive and doing extremely well. It took a lot of time to see the light, the positivity, but I did get there.

This is the one thing I want to emphasize on. The thought that no matter how dire the situation is, how helpless the cause, how unbelievable the circumstances at hand, you can still do it. Life will and must go on. Giving up is not an option. It is not something that I ever learned. Nobody teaches their child to fight off half-body paralysis. But it is something you can bring yourself to do according to the need of the time. There are certain things in life that you have to teach yourself and struggling to stay alive is just one such thing.

I believe that if I can do it, anyone can. I saw nothing but the good in life before the trauma of getting shot. I had a loving family, amazing friends, a doting girlfriend, excellent academic records, and a wonderful job. There was literally nothing lacking in my life. And then suddenly I was thrown in this life I seemed to have no control over. The worst thing was that it was done by a family member, seemingly without motive.

However, I was able to deal with it. I learned to deal with the pain and the hopelessness of the situation without losing hope, and to adjust to my life in such a way that I was able to deal with everything that came my way. What I have learned is that it is ultimately all about your mindset. If you are willing to keep the positivity alive, there is nothing and no one who can bring you down. But you have to have faith in yourself, along with God. Yes, things spiral out of control and may seem like they are completely out of your hands, but you can and will make it. You will come out a victor at the end. I would like to suggest one more thing before telling you about my emotional condition during those days. Learn to differentiate your friends from enemies. It took me a long time to figure out who was being honest with me, and who was using me. But eventually, in time and with experience I realized that true friends don't put blame on you, they don't make you feel bad, and they don't expect you to be perfect all the time.

People who love you let you be and are always there by your side even when you feel like you only deserve to be left alone. But they are there, and so long as you allow them, they will always be there to help you out in the best manner possible. So have courage, stay strong, and remember, you are your biggest motivator. Let no one and nothing come between you and your strong positive mindset. I promise, things will get better in time, just like they did for me. I'm still taking one day at a time, and there are bouts of depression. But for the most part, I am able to function well.

Let yourself heal fully and then plan how you want to take it from there. You will do it. Don't rush, take it one step at a time, and before long, you will see how your journey takes off in leaps and bounds.

Chapter 3- An Inner Battle

My journey down this dark and lonely road started the day my doctors told me that I was paralyzed. Getting shot at leaves an everlasting impact on a person's psyche. Add to that the physical and emotional aftereffects, and it can take forever to overcome the impact. It just isn't just something you can achieve in a short time; t'll take a significant amount of blood, sweat, and tears to get your life back on track again. I don't think there are words to describe just how this incident changed my life.

I was still in the hospital, recuperating from the grueling pain that surged through my legs. The first day I was fully awake and alert in the hospital was January 26th, 2017. The pain coursing through my body was unbearable. At times, it felt like I was being stabbed repeatedly. Other times it felt like there was a snake wrapped around my leg, squeezing me until I'd have to cry out in pain. The agony lasted anywhere from five to thirty minutes. But by the end of each painful episode, I wished for death to ease my suffering.

The doctors finally told me that I was paralyzed. My family was with me at the time, but I never felt so alone. It's not that their company was unwelcome; it was just that they hadn't the slightest clue what I thought at that moment. They could never understand what was going through my mind. I was coming to terms with the fact that I'd be living the rest of my life as a paraplegic. The funny thing is, when you receive such horrible news it takes its sweet time settling in. You are in denial, unable to fully comprehend the gravity of the situation. But it does eventually start to make sense. It took me a day or so to fully understand the impact of paralysis on my life.

The news finally sunk in, and then it hit me like a truck. When I realized I would have to go through hell for the rest of my life, I started weeping and wailing loudly. The tears flooded down my face, and soon my pillowcase was drenched in my tears. Nobody could console me no matter how hard they tried; what could they even say? Would they tell me that it was going to be all right? I already knew nothing ever would. All the prospects and plans I had for my life: my athletics, my academics…everything was going down the drain, right in front of my eyes. And all I could do was sit there and watch it all waste away.

As I wept, a powerful parasite latched on to me…a parasite called depression. Every day, little by little, it sucked the life force out of me. I no longer had the energy to get up or leave my bed. My mind was filled to the brim with hurtful thoughts - no one cared for me, and no one would miss me if I were to disappear. It wanted me to feel nothing but pain, and I cried long and hard. The tears just wouldn't stop flowing.

The thing about depression is that it causes you to behave erratically, even when you know you are unreasonable. That parasite of depression makes you do things and feel things; no sane person would. And while your mind nags at you for being completely irrational, you continue to ignore it. That's because the parasite of depression offers you the sweet, sweet release of death.

My life had changed in a matter of days. It only took one bullet to not only ruin my body and self-image, but also to blow my life apart. I could once to everything on my own, but in a matter of just a days, I went from being ferociously independent to being dependent on others for the most menial of tasks. I would be angry and riddled with a headache all the time. I was mad because of a single thought: *'Why me?'* And for that, neither I nor anyone else, had an answer. My anger gave way to another thought, perhaps the only thing I could think about now that I was paralyzed: *'Would I ever be able to walk again?'* The thought of walking now felt like a dream and a blessing that most people take for granted. They can walk and have no idea just how good they have it. Because for those of us, who have had that privilege taken from them, even everyday tasks are a real struggle.

During my time at the hospital, my mother and brothers confronted the cousin who had shot me. For some reason, he thought it would be a good idea to come and visit me, but my family wasn't having it. After a huge commotion, he was shown the door and warned never to show his face around our family again. But frankly speaking, I could have done with the company. I would have gotten on the path to recovery sooner, had the people I cared about stayed with me.

That's the thing about loved ones, when push comes to shove, a surprisingly small number of them will choose to stand by your side. It is a part of human psyche, I suppose. The people who deserted me now had been the best of friends when I was happy and healthy. However, now that I was in the most trying time of my life, they didn't have the time or inclination to show me the kindness I needed most. Yes, I was sour at how my life had turned out but perhaps with their love and friendship, I could have defeated the evil of depression far sooner. The only time I looked forward to, during the entire day, was the time I spent outside. There was nothing better than fresh air and seeing people all around me, instead of being locked up in my hospital room. I felt like a prisoner in there - all the things I should be doing on my own were now had to be done for me, and that is a great way to make a person feel helpless.

The thought of having to learn to walk all over again angered me to the point where I would get a headache. For many days I couldn't even bring myself to eat. That feeling of helplessness, coupled with the ongoing depression and desertion I was feeling, made it very hard for me to cope with the trauma. Going outside helped me forget it a bit, though.

But even that forgetfulness was short lived as the thoughts of being bound to a wheelchair flooded my mind even more forcefully when I had to go back to my room. As soon as I laid back on that bed, it felt like I was being transported back to the time and place of the shooting. I kept replaying that scene over and over in my head, thinking about what I could have done at that moment to avoid getting shot. As I came up with possible alternatives, I would be brought back to reality by the crushing realization that I was paralyzed for the rest of my life and nothing could be done now. I spent countless sleepless nights, staring into the darkness of my hospital room. Another one of my respites was sports. Despite all of this going on in my head, I was still a huge sports fan. Being paralyzed doesn't stop you from enjoying sports, or at least, it didn't for me. No bullet in the world could have prevented me from loving sports. On the super bowl weekend, my girlfriend stayed with me, while my family visited on Sunday to watch the game with me.

That was a treasured tradition, and it made me really happy that they surrounded me at that time. After a month in hell, I was finally released from the hospital to go home. That car ride was emotional, to say the least. How would I live in this place with this disability? Would I really be able to interact normally with my surroundings? All kinds of questions plagued my already depressed mind. The place I'd called home my entire life seemed strange now, as did my whole life. I kept hitting and bumping into problems. The smallest issues set me off. Seeing anything that reminded me of the time I could use my legs put me back in that helpless mentality back again.

I cried out at the realization that my life would never be the same. When I got home my room was full of teddy bears and balloons. Seeing that, I started crying again. I was an emotional mess. My girlfriend hugged me and told me everything is going to be all right. She encouraged me to cry it all out as it would help me feel better…and it did. I thought being home in my own room would lift my spirits, but all it did was trigger memories of the last time I walked out of my room on my own two legs. This sense of helplessness further fueled my depression. During the day all I would do is lay in bed, and sometimes watch television.

I felt like a kid who had to be taken care of, all over again. I mentioned before that the shot had turned my chronological clock back to being an infant and all of this was just egging me on. My first night at home I didn't rest well at all. I would go to sleep, wake up in two hours, turn on my television to make me fall asleep again, then I would wake back up three hours later and be up for the rest of the day. Around 7 o'clock, I would go outside for some fresh air. I was stressed out because I couldn't sleep, and I was in constant pain. All day I would try to take a nap, but it wasn't to be. Someone always had to be home with me, which again made me feel like a child who had to be supervised at all times.

Some days my brother would come to my house and push me around the neighborhood a couple of times. Other days my friend would visit me, or my girlfriend would come over to keep me company. The pain in my legs would keep me up, and without meaning to, I would cry into the night. Sometimes my crying would be loud enough to wake my mother up, who would come into my room to comfort me. I have to tip my hat to that woman and her spirit. She is the strongest person in my life, because not only did she take care of me, but she also took care of my step-father.

He had cancer. From the moment of his diagnosis to the time he passed, my mother showed an astonishing strength and patience towards the both of us. She would make regular trips to the hospital and home to take care of me. I remembered clearly, that just moments before I got shot, that she had texted me to take the garbage out when I got home. But, of course, I never made it there.

My stepfather had also been a ray of hope in my life. Even while battling cancer, he didn't fail to take care of me whenever he could. Every night, he would stretch my legs out for me, which really helped with my pain. He was an excellent cook, and I loved macaroni and cheese. So my father made it a point to make me my favorite food every other day. My stepfather loved my mom and me. Together they put on a brave face in a time of great heartbreak and sorrow. And my mother retained her strength when he passed away. I wish I could have done more to help her through that tough time. From this entire experience, one thing stood out to me the most. I mentioned above that my road to recovery could have been accelerated had it not been for the people I loved most deserting me, and that is a life lesson I will forever have.

During trying and difficult times, you learn who you can surround yourself with, and who truly cares about you. For me, all the people who claimed to be my friends left me during some of the most challenging days I had ever lived. My circle of friends which, at one time, was huge, slowly got smaller and even my best friend of many years deserted me.

The one person I thought would never let me go, my girlfriend, also said her goodbyes shortly after. About a week into me being at the hospital, I could already sense the change in our relationship. I guess it was a blessing in disguise that I got to know who really loved me. She started making up excuses to not come see me. Sometimes she would complain about my friends and family coming to see me while I was in the hospital. She used to say things like *"There are way too many people here, and I feel suffocated. I'm going home."* However, soon I realized that she just didn't understand that I liked having people around me because it was the only thing that kept my mind off the pain. She grew heartless towards me eventually. She lost all empathy for me. Often, she would tell me I was aggravating my situation by overthinking, or she'd leave if I didn't stop crying. The pain was unbearable, and all I wanted was to feel still loved. According to her, I was clingy but what would you expect from a person who had been paralyzed in the prime of his life?

It had only been a few days since I had moved back home from the hospital when I felt a definite change in her behavior towards me. She started saying negative things to me to make me feel small. That was her way of trying to get out of the relationship. She should have come to me and told me that she was still young and that was not ready to take on the responsibilities of a paralyzed boyfriend. But instead, she chose to badmouth me to our friends, telling them that she hated putting my wheelchair in the car when I could have walked just fine.

I would never have thrown all the things I had done for her in her face, because all of that came from the heart. However, it hurt to see how a person I once thought was going to be by my side forever was suddenly choosing to leave me alone. Yes, my circumstances were different and difficult to understand, but I never thought our love would change. The difference between her and me was that I really, truly loved her. If this situation has taught me anything, it's that people, especially your loved ones, will leave you high and dry in your time of need.

Before my incident, my relationship with God wasn't the best. Just like most young people, I didn't think about religion a lot. But that changed now that I had time alone with myself, and I was in so much pain. I had realized that relying on humans isn't the best thing to do. You see, people always leave, but God is there for us. No matter what you are going through, He will always be present, listening and helping you out. I had never thought about that before. It was only when everyone left, did I realize that there was still a constant presence, fighting for me and willing me to defeat the evil parasite of depression. I got to work, rebuilding my relationship with God.

Before I got shot, I would say a short prayer before I left the house. It was more of a formality, which my mother had mandated. That was about the only time I would pray outside the church. And even going to church wasn't on my weekly agenda, and I never understood the word of God. The stress of my predicament caused me to question him about why He let this happen to me. What did I do to deserve it? Why had He allowed me to live? Just like all human beings, I asked Him these questions, not understanding what wisdom He may have had in this. I didn't thank Him when I was in good health, and I resented Him when I faced a difficult time. I was down on my luck, and loss of faith was inevitable, given the circumstances surrounding me and lack of it before.

During the earlier days of my horrible suffering, I had lost all my faith because I just couldn't understand why. Why was it that those of us who have the most to lose, and who don't do others any harm, are taken down? My cousin, who shot me, remained in perfect health and high spirits. Nothing happened to him. And I, who was my parent's pride and joy, who was working two jobs and had graduated high school, I got shot. It hadn't even been a year since I graduated high school, I was working two jobs, and I had also stopped going out as much. I was focused on building myself, saving as much money as I could so I could start my business in a few years, and maintaining my relationships at the time. I lost so much, so quickly that I didn't have time to process it all. But through God's grace, I found Him. And soon enough, I started to become accustomed to my new life. Therapy worked somewhat, and while the paralysis showed more improvement, much of my pain subsided. I began to renew my relationship with God. He eventually became the source of my strength and the power of my life. I was motivated and determined to get my life back on the right track.

Chapter 4- Finding Hope

God has blessed each of us with special abilities, but we have to push ourselves to explore these gifts and utilize them to the fullest. We all have aspirations and dreams that motivate us to reach for more and to achieve unbelievably difficult tasks. These accomplishments can brighten up the darkest of days for many of us, but for me they were bittersweet.

Since that fateful day that I'd been shot, my life became very different from what it had been earlier. My peace and happiness seemed to be lightyears away from me. I was learning to function in my current state. In all honesty, it was very sad of affairs, and I had to go through it all because of the malice of one person. I was reduced to hoping that I would be able to resume the essential functions of life, while others my age were reaching for their goals and dreams.

They were excelling at difficult feats, while taking care of myself had become the most challenging task in my life. At some point, I had shared goals and dreams with them. However now, our paths had been separated forever. It was insanely difficult, learning how to live that life, and live it happily. I could see what I had lost. It was my freedom, my expression and my will to live. I was worse than a six-year-old. Feeding, bathing, washing were all monumental challenges and bit-by-bit I had to relearn these tasks. I hated being dependent on others. It was not great for my self-esteem. It was just so hard to learn to be better. I realized that my depressed and dejected mindset was just as responsible for my misery as my condition was. In my uphill battle to recover, I started working towards a positive mindset; I started saying *'I can'* instead of *'I can't'* when I felt like I wanted to give up on doing something.

I know that it sounds very simple, but it works.

Your mind is a powerful tool, and it has great power over your body. It tells every muscle what to do. Once you've conquered your mind, you can conquer yourself as well. This is key to your happiness, no matter what physical state you are in. Negative thoughts will only drag you down instead of uplifting you; I learned this the hard way. Good things will happen when you speak positively. Speaking life into existence is always the key. You can do anything in life if you put your mind to it. I learned to tell myself that I would get out of this situation.

Initially, I didn't know what to do. However, a few months later I had a newfound resolve to be better than my situation. I was capable of living this life and become better as a person. The next step was to take my physical therapy seriously. It was pure torture to be in physical therapy. My muscles felt like they were being ripped apart, fiber from fiber, but I was determined to do this right. It worked wonders and pulled me out of depression. Ever since I took the initiative to stand up against my negativity, I had become a much happier person. I was at peace with myself. The motivation was coming from everywhere, especially from my physical therapy instructors.

They were great. They always show me my chart and how I did the last time I was in therapy. They kept track of my strengths and weakness. Anything that I felt I couldn't do, my instructors motivated me to do it. I figured that since I was fighting this battle alone I should give it my all. No one was coming to save me. I put all my energy into learning how to walk again. I pushed myself and got better results in therapy. Every time that I went to therapy I loved receiving good news about my results, and how much better I was doing. Of course, each of the sessions was more grueling than the last, but that didn't stop me from pushing myself to the limit. I was going to do this thing, come what may. It was a year since I had been diagnosed with paralysis. This fact alone could have debilitated and depressed me for days had I lived with my previous mindset. But now, I didn't care to dwell on the past. I was determined to walk no matter what it took. I knew that only I could control how I feel and what I do. I surrounded myself with nothing except positivity. My prayers became my number one focus, and then came my physical therapy.

My therapist became my friend, and my relationship with God was now rock-solid. I started going to church every Sunday with my mother. It was a lovely feeling to be in the embrace of God, as I sang His praises and listened to His word. Many times I felt that they were talking to me, about me. This strengthened my resolve. I enjoyed the new outlook on my situation, no matter how grim it was in reality. My life, even though difficult, was quite a blessing.

Everything started to make sense to me now. I was ready for the change. Irrespective of the obstacles in front of me, I was determined to make this situation better. Eventually, my physical and mental health improved. As my body regained its strength, so did my mental health. God had kept me going when I had given up on myself. My family and friends rescued me and helped me lived with dignity. I appreciate them for being there for me every step of the way. If things hadn't transpired the way they did, I would never have been able to tell my real friends from the fake ones, and for that, I will always be thankful. My real friends were a greater blessing than I could have ever asked for. I was never one to lie down and do nothing. That's just not who I am. I knew that I couldn't escape this situation and nothing could become of it except death. I did not even want to go for my therapy. I wanted to die.

My brothers helped me realize that I was so much better than that. They reminded me just how much I was capable of. In a way, my victories are theirs as much as they are mine. They helped me remember that I wanted to get married, have kids, and watch them go to college one day. The love and kindness that my mother gave me kept reminding me of my aspirations and hopes. There have been times where she had to call off work because I wasn't in my right mind. Sometimes the pain would be too unbearable. I was lucky to have this support system. They helped me maintain my optimistic streak when things got dark.

I had to be healthy for them as they prayed by my side. My uncle Michael and Aunt Bobbie, were two people who I am genuinely grateful for, always just a call away. They prayed for me, checked in on me, and brought me supplies whenever I needed any. When I returned from the hospital, and my mom returned to work, Auntie Chess took over and helped me out. In the year 2017, I had to return to the hospital as I was about to die. Things had deteriorated to the extent that it could have been life-threatening.

I returned to my home after five days, and by this time it was Christmas. I was still in the wheelchair, but with time, I believed I would walk again. I'm grateful for everything that I have, and I am blessed to have God by my side. Although sometimes I do think anyone else in the world had it as bad as I did, but then I am reminded of the fact that I had my faith. God was my biggest motivator, and he showed me the way through the tough times.

If I can make it, anyone can. You can do anything you want to do, but it's always going to be up to you to take the first step. That's what I tell myself every day when I look in the mirror and see my doubts. I push them away, I know I'll walk again; I just know it.

"Your imagination is your preview of life's coming attractions."

-Albert Einstein

Your thoughts can sometimes be your enemy. They can be a hindrance to your mind's potential. Hold yourself above the hate, spite, intolerance, tiredness or confusion. Have trust in the way of the Lord. He's shaping the play for you. Be hungry, strive for His blessings, and wait for what He has in store for you, and He will reward you with more. The secret to living a satisfying life is believing in Him and motivating yourself even when you don't want to.

Never utter negative or discouraging remarks about yourself, because you will only manifest this negativity into your life. So think of ways to take charge of your life. Know that you can make it better. Understand that God has given you the choices and it's up to you to select the right thing for you. Compile new strategies to bring you closer to your destiny. Stop living your fears; that's the reason you haven't leveled up yet. You can't be afraid to find out what's next. Satisfaction comes with knowing you tried to persevere through all your circumstances.

"The journey of a thousand miles begins with one step."

-Lao

I see God has blessed me so much. I shouldn't have let my faith down for the little time that I did, and I regret that immensely. Once I changed my mindset and became more positive; things started to happen for me. I've been receiving better results in physical therapy, and I even found a girl. She motivates me in ways that you couldn't imagine. She helped me build my self-confidence, which just so happened to be one of the most crucial parts of my progress. She knew just the way to make me feel good and take care of me. My family is a big fan of her as well. We respect and love one another unconditionally.

I guess what they say is true. *'What doesn't kill you simply makes you stronger.'*

I'm honestly ready for all the challenges life could bring in the future and even now. I'm thankful for my health and the ones who stood by me through everything. Without anyone in your corner, some challenges tend to be hard to overcome. However, it's incredible how we gather the courage to overcome those problems. I'm also grateful for what I know now. All the people in my life who deserted me, all the painful surgeries I had to endure, all those nights spent in the hospital wondering what was going to happen… I've decided that I can help people like me. I can't live with myself knowing that there are people out there who are going through exactly what I went through and they are in a position much worse than I was in. I want to motivate and speak to people about getting through depression and how you can overcome it all. I have decided to make it my aim in life to help as many people as I can.

Even though I was deserted by the ones I thought were my real friends, I was also blessed with better people who replaced them. On second thought, they had always been there. However, I think I took them for granted. I realize that not everyone has the blessing of love in their lives. I want to motivate them and tell them that it's okay. You can defeat your circumstances. Promise that you will keep pushing yourself to success. My recovery has been tremendous so far, even though there's still an uphill battle. Your recovery will be great too. Just believe in yourself and never give up.

Chapter 5- Road to Betterment

I feel as if I have gone through a lot of pain, suffering, trials and tribulation in my short life. However, I have come to a very simple conclusion. All of those sufferings and pains accomplished exactly what they were supposed to; they made me a better person. The most important thing I understand right now is that life is incredibly short. We cannot live it within the cage constructed by our own minds. I have said over and over again that the power our minds have over our body is immensely considerable, and it can always set us free. However, it works the other way too.

Here is another way my ordeal could have panned out. I got shot by my cousin because of jealousy. He wanted to take my life just because I was doing much better than he was and he was not okay with that. It was such a petty reason to shoot me. I could not understand it. I will not lie and be all holier-than-thou and say that the thought of revenge never crossed my mind. I could have hurt him in some way and made the score even. Nobody would have even blamed me even if I did. But the simple fact was that I was better than him. Even without my legs, I was still the better person. I was the bigger man. I know that it sounds cocky, but it is a fact. The entire reason he shot me was that he feared that I was doing very well in my life. Shooting him would have made me exactly like him, and that would have been a harder thing to live with than forgiving him. Ephesians 4:31-32 says: *"Get rid of all bitterness, rage and anger, brawling and slander, along with every form of malice. Be kind and compassionate to one another, forgiving each other, just as in Christ God forgave you."*

My cousin practically took away my entire life yet when I was down in the dumps, at the lowest point of my life, I could see no hope. Don't misunderstand me. When I was going through the most perilous moments of my life, I actually thought I wouldn't make it. This is another thing that most people don't realize. When they hear the story of a person who has been through much worse than they have; they think that those people are made of different stuff than they have been.

That is not so. In a way, I would have actually been the worse man had I followed that route. The thing is, going through those moments of immense pain and suffering were actually a blessing in disguise. I learned that humans are actually much more resilient than we make ourselves to be. We are the creations of God, and Jesus died for all of our sins. It is very important to understand that no matter what pains or trials befall you in life, they are nothing more than what you can handle.

God is ever loving, and ever merciful to us. He would never give us anything more than we could handle. I know that most people seem to think otherwise. They have been through so much that they seem to lose their grip on reality. They retreat into their minds to the point that it is almost impossible for them ever to find the way out. While I do not mean to demean their suffering, I believe it is important to think about those people who have it much worse than us. Now do you really think that of all those people? That not even one of them could conquer what they though to be unconquerable? That all of them should let their situations dictate their state of mind?

The only thing stopping you from being content is your own mindset. The fact of the matter is that most people seem to believe no matter what the situation, they could always be in a better situation. Most of us are always looking at people who are doing better than us. No matter how good we have it, there is always someone who has it better. We are looking towards them and hoping and working towards what they have. Let me ask you this question: why is it that we have to have what other people have? Why can we not be happy with what we have? Most people would answer this question with something like, 'because what we have isn't enough.'

Consider this though, what you have in your life could be what most people hope and dream to have in their entire lives. This especially applies for most of the people who are reading this book. It is an acceptable assumption that you have a place to live, a car, food on your plate and most importantly your arms and legs. You are in good health, breathing normally, and you are living your life respectably. That puts you among the luckiest people on the planet.

People in parts of Africa are starving. People in Hiroshima and Nagasaki are born with defects. People in Palestine and Syria live every day of their lives knowing that it could be their last. They live with the weight of what has happened to their mothers, fathers, sons, daughters, wives, husbands, cousins, relatives, teachers, students, literally every person they meet. They don't know if it will be the last time they see them. So what is our suffering compared to theirs?

Again, this in no way means that what we are going through in our lives is not substantial, because it is not like that. The problems we go through in our lives are real and they have very real consequences. The reason for pointing this out was to make us understand that things we go through should not have the power to disturb our happiness. I know it sounds silly, but bear with me.

If we think about how good we have it, compared to other people living elsewhere on the planet, then maybe that just puts things into perspective. It doesn't mean that you stop trying to solve those problems. It just means that we should keep in mind that those problems aren't the end of the world for us. This is the mindset I was talking about. The mindset that no matter what type of situation you are going through, you firmly believe that you will come out of it. You may not come out unscathed; your personality and outlook on life may be changed entirely, but you will come out. If you achieve that mindset, nothing in your life can ever make you want to wish that you were anybody other than who you are, regardless of the circumstances.

When my cousin shot me, I was well on the way to becoming one of the most successful men in my family. After the shooting, however, all the people I associated with, who I thought would be there for me through thick and thin, left me to fend for myself. I've mentioned that during my hospital stay, the only times I was thrilled was when people would come to visit me. However, it didn't take long for them to show me their real colors. The biggest hurt and betrayal of all was that my girlfriend left me.

This is another thing I want to talk about. It was a very real heartbreak, and that was hard to come back from. When someone you never imagined would leave you does leave you, you start to actually wonder if there is something really wrong with you. You start to think that you are unlovable, that you don't deserve to be loved. I stress on this because that is what most people think when they are abandoned. They don't even consider the possibility that there might have been something wrong with the person who left them. It is always self-blame that takes over their mentality. 'I was not good enough to be with them.' 'It was my fault that they are leaving me.' 'I don't deserve to burden anyone with myself.' The fact of the matter is: if you are with someone who makes you think any of these things, you shouldn't be with them in the first place. That is because you are practically telling yourself that you aren't worth any love, affection or companionship and let me tell you this straight up; that is not the case with anyone in the world.

True love isn't the idealistic picture that Hollywood and romantic novels paint. Those novels and movies show, more or less, the same thing. A man falls in love with a woman, or vice versa. They go through a series of minor difficulties that have no real world effect whatsoever, and it always ends the same way; with the girl in the guy's arms as they reach their happily ever after. In the real world, that never happens. The reality differs greatly from what we to for entertainment

When you are with your partner, you aren't just with them when they are happy or healthy. You are with them when they are in the lowest point of their lives. You are with them when they lose themselves in their grief. This is because when you fell in love with them, you embraced every part of them, even the ones they hate to admit they have. When you are with someone like that, it is important to know that while they will be there for you through thick and thin, at the end of the day they are still human. They have needs, just as you have needs. Everything that goes for them, also goes for you. If they are with you through your lowest point, it is your responsibility to make that worth it for them. To understand this, I will give you an example that you have probably heard before. This is the example of Connor McGregor, and his wife, Dee Devlin. The story of Connor McGregor and his wife, though filled with hardships and tribulations is one that is true, at its core. Here is what Connor says about his wife.

"We've been together for more than eight years. We lived in Ireland, thirty kilometers from Dublin, in a rented apartment on €188 unemployment benefit. I had no job because I spent all my time at the gym. I believed that I would be champion and she did too. Despite our lack of money, she got me to eat right and keep my daily regime. She dedicated herself to it. After coming home exhausted she always said, "Connor, it's okay. You can do it."'

-Connor McGregor

That was a real world problem. Connor and his wife were going through really hard times. Do you honestly think that Dee Devlin didn't think that she would be better off with someone else? Someone who could actually support her financially, someone who didn't need as much looking after as Connor did? It is impossible to assume that, but actions speak louder than words. Even through that, she stayed with Connor, because she actually loved him and believed in him.

For you to deserve that level of commitment from someone, you must first actually be that someone for them. If I look at my own example, I would like to think that even when I was down in the dumps and felt alone, there was some part of me that knew that I would always get through this. I was paralyzed, that did not mean that I was any less of a person than I was before.

Some of you who are going through trying times might believe that this is a very naïve way to look at things. However, that doesn't mean that it's not right or any less true. For your partner to accept you as you are, that is a true test of loyalty. If they are to leave you, that doesn't mean that you should hold that against them. It just means that they were not ready to do that, and it is completely understandable. If you're still holding on to grudges, you can never fully recover and set yourself in a mindset that will bring you happiness and peace. The grudges you hold will bring you nothing except a mentality that will render you incapable of happiness and growth. Holding onto grudges against someone who did you wrong is kind of like holding onto a sack filled with rocks while climbing a mountain. It will just slow you down. It is completely useless. Many people think that letting go of grudges against people is hard. They seem to be under the impression that letting go of grudges makes them less of a person. To them, forgiving someone who did them wrong would mean that they are unable to make them feel the way they did.

However, think of it this way, you can either spend your time and energy on thinking up ways to take revenge, or you can move on knowing that they don't deserve your energy and time. If you are under the impression that it will make you any less of a person, then know that this is much harder to do than holding a grudge. 'Resentment and grudges are things we dare not collect in our spirits, for they will spoil and rot, producing poison that will contaminate our words as our actions.' Even if all of that isn't enough to convince you that holding onto grudges does nobody any hard except you, then let me quote a couple of verses from the Bible. ***Romans***

12:17-21 says: "Repay no one evil for evil, but give thought to do what is honorable in the sight of all. If possible, so far as it depends on you, live peaceably with all. Beloved, never avenge yourselves, but leave it to the wrath of God, for it is written, *"Vengeance is mine, I will repay, says the Lord."* On the contrary, *"if your enemy is hungry, feed him; if he is thirsty, give him something to drink; for by so doing you will heap burning coals on his head."* Do not be overcome by evil, but overcome evil with good."

If you read this verse, you might think that God is commanding you to forgive the people whom you hold grudges against. However, the real reason that it seems like that is because God knows how humans think. He knows that even though you could work this out on your own, you still won't do it. That is why He commands you to do it. The fact is that following God's instructions on how to live your life will liberate you on a level you could never have imagined. That is what I have gleaned through my pain and suffering.

At the end of day, when everyone has left you, you realize that no matter how many people desert you, God will always be there for you. Another really important thing that you need when getting through a tough time is people. Even though love and hope will always be there by your side, you do need someone to be physically present for you. For me, I was lucky enough to have my mother, brothers and relatives by my side. However, not everyone is as blessed as I am in that regard. Even so, what I said above still applies. God never gives you trouble that you can't handle. That being said, you need to understand that you are really very strong. You are resilient and you are unbreakable.

I know that at that point in your life when you are at your lowest it is hard to believe that. It is so easy to give up and just accept the state you are in. But that will achieve nothing. The purpose of life is happiness. In reality you will never rest until you have achieved that. So, never give up, never give in and always know that by the blessing of God, you will always be able to achieve that!

One *Step*
At A *Time*

This is a story of a strong man with a strong power of will. A man who was shot in the back and miraculously survived only to end up being partially paralyzed. In his book *"One Step at a Time"*, Mario has shared his experience of how he survived through the tragic damage to his spine by a bullet, yet refused to give up and keep on fighting the odds. With the passage of time, he learns to forgive people regardless of what they had done to him and never lose hope of getting a new life. This allows Mario to live a peaceful life and the results in finding the love of his life who accepts the way he is.

Mario Simmons

www.ingramcontent.com/pod-product-compliance
Lightning Source LLC
Chambersburg PA
CBHW021937170626
46807CB00007B/3153